the Dragon Cant

Written by **James Dongweck** Illustrated by **Joe Baker**

Golden Monkey Publishing LLC

Old Saybrook CT

GOLDEN MONKEY

Published by Golden Monkey Publishing, LLC

Text Copyright © 2003 James Dongweck
Illustrations Copyright © 2003 Joe Baker
All rights reserved. Published by Golden Monkey Publishing, LLC
For information about permission to reproduce selections
from this book write to :

Permissions
Golden Monkey Publishing, LLC
24 Meadowood Lane
Old Saybrook, CT 06475
www.goldenmonkeypublishing.com

Dongweck, James.
    The dragon cant / by James Dongweck ; illustrated by
  Joe Baker. -- 1st ed.
    p. cm.
    SUMMARY : Who will save the small, peaceful village
  besieged by the evil and hungry Dragon Cant?
    Audience : Grades K-3.
    ISBN 0-9719632-0-7

    1. Dragons--Juvenile fiction. [1.Dragons--Fiction.]
  I. Baker, Joe, 1974 - II. Title

PZ7.D71654Dra 2003   [E]
                  QBI33-1135

Library of Congress Control Number: 2003090404

More Joe Baker paintings can be seen at www.joebaker.net

Paintings in the book are oils on paper.

Printed in China

First Edition

10 9 8 7 6 5 4 3 2

Once there was a small, peaceful village resting against the base of a hill. In that village everyone worked, played, and lived without a care in the world.

Until...

One dark day, the Dragon Cant crawled out of the surrounding forest, wrapped itself around the top of the hill, and stared down at the village with hungry eyes.

"What are we to do?" the frightened villagers asked each other. "A Dragon looms above us. It will eat us all."

"We know what to do," said a small girl standing beside her brother.

"Not now, children," said a villager. "You're interrupting us."

The townsfolk ran to the guard at the front gate and asked him, "What are you going to do about the Dragon?"

"Me? I can't do a thing," said the Sergeant of the Gate. "My knees are shaking, I am so afraid."

When the Dragon Cant heard this, it raised a wicked eyebrow, smiled a toothy smile, and slithered a little bit down the hill toward the village.

□□□

So the townsfolk hurried to the Captain in the barracks and asked him, "What are you going to do about the Dragon?"

"I can't do a thing," said the Captain. "It will eat me in two bites."

Chomp chomp, whispered the Dragon Cant when it heard its name again.

For a second time, it slyly inched a little closer to the village.

□□□

So the townsfolk fled to the castle and called to the General, "What are you going to do about the Dragon?"

"I can't do a thing," said the General, who peeked out from behind the drawbridge. "I am too old and too tired."

Delightful, they're calling my name again, said the Dragon Cant, as it crept ever closer to the base of the hill.

□□□

So the townsfolk cried out to the Queen in the tower, "What are you going to do about the Dragon?"

"I can't do a thing," said the Queen, who hid behind a rosebush on her balcony. "It is too big and too dangerous."

The Dragon twitched its tail in pleasure.

So the townsfolk huddled together, worried and afraid about the Dragon who lurked just above their village.

"Well, I can't bake any bread," said the Baker. "Not with the Dragon up there."

The Dragon Cant stretched its claws in anticipation.

"Well, I can't sew any clothes," said the Tailor. "Not with that Dragon above us."

Cant's tongue flicked between its teeth.

□□□

"Well, I can't fix any homes," said the Carpenter. "Not with a Dragon on its way to eat us all."

The Dragon snapped its jaws, just to get them ready.

With each "can't" the Dragon heard, it slid around boulders and darted between trees, inching closer and closer to the village.

□□□

"I can't" this, and "I can't" that, said the townsfolk on and on and on and on — until the Dragon Cant's horn-crowned head snaked through the open gate.

Steam hissed from its nose and fire flew from its mouth. It only needed to hear its name called out one more time and Cant could enter the village.

Allllmost theeeere, said the Dragon.

The Dragon Cant grinned a horrible grin and raised its front claw. A terrified farmer opened his mouth –

"WAIT!" cried a tiny voice.

The village fell into a startled silence. Angry puffs of smoke snorted from the Dragon's nose.

"We CAN do something," shouted the little girl.

WHAT? hissed the Dragon, and it froze in its place.

The townsfolk spun around
to see the girl and boy, who
had climbed atop the
statue of a horse in the
village square.

"What did you say?" called
out the Queen.

"We said, we can do
something," replied the girl.

NO! snarled Cant.

"First, we can close the
front gate," said the boy.

The Dragon reared onto its
hind legs and roared
in anger.

"I know we can do even
more," said the girl.

Cant struggled and strained
to enter the village,
but it couldn't.

"Yes, yes," said the Sergeant. "We can close the gate."

Not that terrible WORD, bellowed the Dragon Cant, and it staggered back a step.

"And we can man the walls," said the Captain.

"And we can raise the army," said the General.

"And we can fight the Dragon," said the Queen.

"And I can bake bread for the soldiers," said the Baker.

"And I can sew their uniforms," said the Tailor.

"And I can fix damages to the town," said the Carpenter.

"We can" this, and "We can" that, said the townsfolk on and on and on and on.

With each "can" the Dragon Cant heard, it was forced farther and farther away from the village. It blew smoke. It spit fire. It roared into the air. It even clawed into the ground. But the Dragon Cant couldn't move one scale, one tooth, or one whisker closer to the village.

□□□

Soon, the dragon stumbled backward over the hill, rolled down to the edge of the trees, and tumbled deeper and deeper into the forest. Little by little, Cant faded from view, until only its faintly glowing eyes peeked between the leaves.

Finally, the eyes blinked... and disappeared.

And from that day on the Dragon Cant was never seen near the village ever again.